JUST A BAD DAY

BY GINA AND MERCER MAYER

Westport, Connecticut

When I woke up this morning, it was raining.
I knew it was going to be a bad day.

I wanted a bowl of Sugar Krispies for breakfast, but the box was empty. I had to have oatmeal instead. Yuck!

I looked for my favorite shirt, but
it was dirty. I had to wear a shirt
I didn't even like.

I wanted to watch cartoons on TV, but they were all reruns. This really was a bad day.

So I decided to paint a picture.
But my sister had left the tops off
my paints, and they were all dried up.

I wanted to play with my new truck, but my dad
had stepped on it by accident and broken the wheel.

So I decided to put my puzzle together instead.
Some of the pieces were missing.
This was such a bad day.

I asked Mom if I could play in the rain.
But she said, "It's too wet."

So I let the dog in to play. But Mom made me
put him back out because he was too wet.

I said, "But I'm bored."
Mom said, "Why don't you play
a game with your sister?"

I tried to play cards with my sister.
She threw them all over the room.

Then we played chase, but Mom made us stop because we were too noisy.

"Please play something that's a little
more quiet," Mom said.

So we colored in our coloring books. I got mad
at my sister because she broke some of my crayons.
She cried. Mom yelled at both of us.
Boy! Was this a bad day!

Then it stopped raining. But Mom wouldn't let me go outside because it was so muddy.

And my baseball game was canceled
because the field was too wet.
This was the worst day ever.

Then my dad came home. He had a surprise for me.
It was a truck, just like the one he had broken.
He brought my sister a surprise, too.

Today was just a bad day.
But at least it had a happy ending.